# Big Band Night

## Created by Keith Chapman

First published in Great Britain by HarperCollins Children's Books in 2007

1 3 5 7 9 10 8 6 4 2
ISBN-13: 978-0-00-722597-2
ISBN: 0-00-722597-0

Based on the television series *Fifi and the Flowertots* and the
original script 'Big Band Night' by Wayne Jackman.
© Chapman Entertainment Limited 2007

Printed and bound in China

# Big Band Night

HarperCollins *Children's Books*

It was the day of the Flowertot Concert and Fifi was helping Bumble practise his drumming.

"I'm really excited about playing in the band tonight," Bumble said, waving his drumsticks around. "Listen!"

Over on the other side of the garden, Stingo was having a bit of a snooze outside his Apple Tree House when...

BANG BANG
BOOM BOOM
BANG!

"Stonking Strawberries!" he yelped. "What was that?" He grabbed his telescope and looked out over the garden. "Bumble playing his rotten drums!" Stingo muttered. "Something needs to be done..."

As Fifi arrived in the clearing, everyone was
busy setting up for the concert.
"Hi everyone!" she waved.
Fifi was so excited,
this concert was going
to be the best!

Bumble was bashing away on his drums when he realised he had some visitors. Stingo and Slugsy were stood behind him and Stingo did not look very happy at all.

"Oh, hello Stingo," Bumble said nervously. "What do you want?"

"What do I want?" yelled Stingo. "I want you to stop making such a racket and disturbing my beauty sleep!"

Bumble picked up his drumsticks.
"But I need to practise for the
concert tonight!" he said.

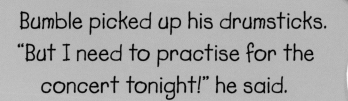

"The what?" asked Stingo. "I'm
going to be disturbed all night
by a noisy concert? Slugsy, we've
got to put a stop to this."

But Slugsy was too busy
swaying to the beat.
"But I like concertsss bosss!"
he said, dancing from side to
side. Stingo gave him a hard
stare. "Sorry bosss"
he muttered.

On the other side of the garden, the Flowertots had almost finished putting the stage together.

"Did you put up the posters, Fifi?" asked Violet.

"Fiddly Flowerpetals!" cried Fifi, dropping her microphone. Violet and Primrose looked at each other and laughed.

"I'm sorry everyone," Fifi said. "Don't worry though, I'll drive round in Mo and make an announcement." She plucked a daffodil trumpet and used it as a loud-hailer so everyone in Flowertot Garden could hear her.

"Come to the Flowertot Concert! Great music tonight!" she called.

Pip was scooting along when he heard the announcement. "Wow, I'll be there!" he called.

Aunt Tulip and Grubby were picking strawberries. "Sweet Potatoes, Grubby loves singing!"

Webby was meditating in her web. "Ooh, I love concerts," she smiled.

Stingo and Slugsy hid as Bumble buzzed off
to help the other Flowertots.
"He's gone," whispered Stingo. "Slugsy, grab
those drums!"
Slugsy started hauling the drums away
while Stingo looked around the garden.
"I might just have a look around to
see if Bumble has left any honey
for me... ah-ha!"

At the stage, Violet, Primrose
and Poppy were practising their dance
routine when Fifi came pootling up in Mo.

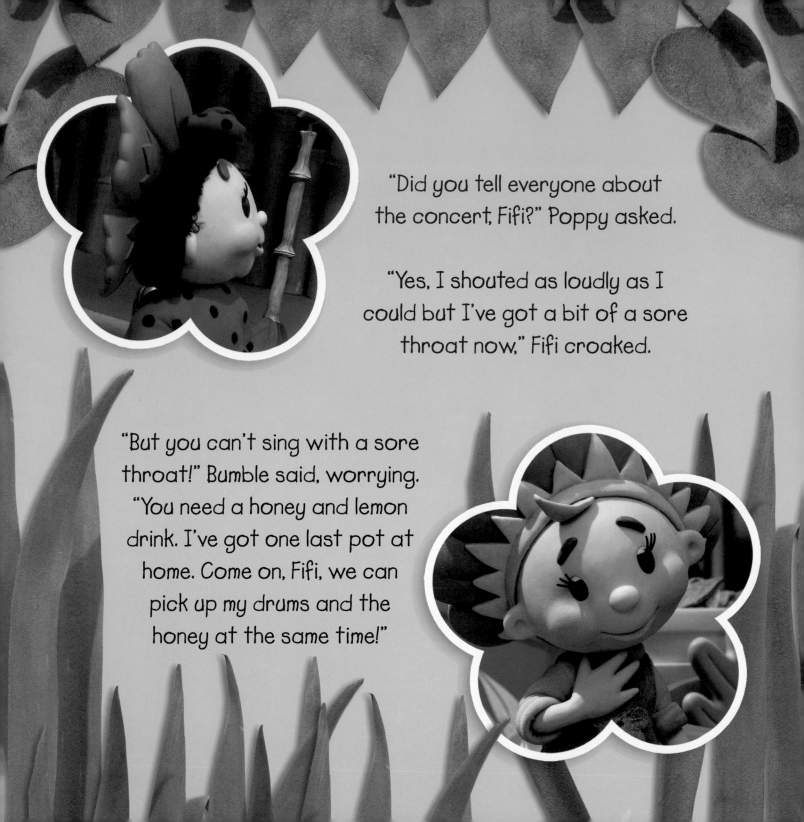

"Did you tell everyone about the concert, Fifi?" Poppy asked.

"Yes, I shouted as loudly as I could but I've got a bit of a sore throat now," Fifi croaked.

"But you can't sing with a sore throat!" Bumble said, worrying. "You need a honey and lemon drink. I've got one last pot at home. Come on, Fifi, we can pick up my drums and the honey at the same time!"

But when Fifi and Bumble arrived at
Honeysuckle House, there was no
honey to be seen and his drums
were missing!

"Oh no!" wailed Bumble.
"We'll have to cancel the concert!"

Stingo buzzed down outside his Apple Tree House with his stolen jar of honey. "Sting-a-Ling!" he chuckled. "I get a delicious jar of honey and a quiet night's sleep! Where did you hide the drums, Slugsy?"

Slugsy pointed happily to the big pile of drums in the corner of the deck. "Ta-Da!" he said happily.

Stingo was stunned. "What did you hide them here for?" he panicked.

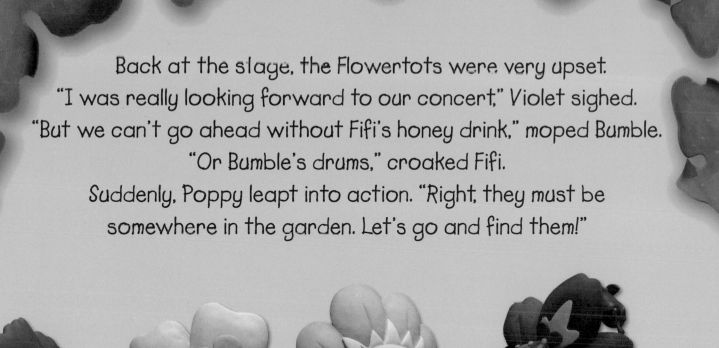

Back at the stage, the Flowertots were very upset.
"I was really looking forward to our concert," Violet sighed.
"But we can't go ahead without Fifi's honey drink," moped Bumble.
"Or Bumble's drums," croaked Fifi.
Suddenly, Poppy leapt into action. "Right, they must be
somewhere in the garden. Let's go and find them!"

Stingo
was trying to
find somewhere else
to hide Bumble's drums
when the Flowertots arrived.
"I don't care where they go,"
Stingo yelled.
"Just hide them!"
But it was too late!

"My drums!" cried Bumble as they fell out of the tree and crashed to the floor.

"Sssorry, Bumble," said Slugsy shyly. "It was Ssstingo's idea. He told me to hide the drumsss while he took the honey – ooopsss!"

The Flowertots were very, very angry!

"Rotten Raspberries." said Stingo.

With the drums back where they belonged it
was soon time for the concert to begin.
Fifi sipped her honey drink and was right
as rain and ready to sing!

As the band took to the stage, the crowd noticed a new member on cymbals. It was Stingo. The other Tots had decided the best punishment would be for him to join in their concert, whether he liked it or not!

"I didn't know you were in the band, bosss!" waved Slugsy.

The Flowertot Band were a huge hit! Even Stingo started to enjoy himself, even if he did jump every time Bumble hit his drums.

After playing all their songs, they all jumped off the stage to enjoy a plate of honey sandwiches with their friends.

# Make Your Own Drums

Drums are so much fun. Remember not to bang them too hard though or Stingo might come and take them away!

You will need:

* Some large cans
* Several layers of coloured paper
* Some glue
* Some rubber bands
* Colouring in things
* Pencils with rubbers on the end as drum sticks
* Wax paper or vinyl

1. Cut the coloured paper so that it is as tall as the cans and long enough to wrap around it.

2. Decorate one side of the paper using paints or crayons

4. Cut circles from the wax paper or vinyl at least 1 inch bigger than the cans and place the circles over the cans.

5. Fold over the excess paper. Attach the circles to the cans with the rubber bands. Make this tight, so you can start banging your drums!